2/20

D1304056

For Tom

Thanks for believing in me and for
being a superb doggy dad.

www.mascotbooks.com

DARCY & DAISY: THE CHRISTMAS PUPPY

For more information, please contact:
Mascot Books
620 Herndon Parkway, Suite 320
Herndon, VA 20170
info@mascotbooks.com

Library of Congress Control Number: 2019905219

CPSIA Code: PRT0719A
ISBN-13: 978-1-64543-011-7

Printed in the United States

DARCY & DAISY
The Christmas Puppy

KARiN HOViNG

Illustrated by Alycia Pace

MASCOT BOOKS

Hi, I'm Darcy! I was just a tiny fellow when my family brought me to this green house on top of the hill and told me it was my forever home. That means I get to stay here always and forever!

I get scrumptious treats and squeaky toys and lots of human kisses.

I know I'm lucky to have a forever home.

There's just one thing I want:
a friend to play with!

My human sister Delaney loves spending time with me, but I'm never any good at her games. I'd rather wrestle. I'm also not convinced I'm a princess or a rock star, but good luck telling her that!

My cat brother Big Red can jump really high and open doors by himself. He loves bird watching and speaks a strange hissing language. He seemed like a perfect playmate, but when I tried to play with him…*ouch!*

Skittles is my other brother. He's much smaller than Big Red, and he can fit a TON of cereal in his cheeks! I thought he'd be a great playmate, but he likes to keep to himself. I love when he goes in his exercise bubble, but he can't get away from me fast enough!

I love all my siblings, but none of them are the perfect playmate for me.

One day in the summer, my human mom and dad brought a wriggly box with holes in it home. **What was inside?** New playmates for me?

When Mom opened the box, two baby kittens poked their heads out. They were like mini Big Reds! I ran up to say hello, but Mom told me to keep my distance. The kittens had been found on the streets of the city all alone and needed medicine to help them get strong.

The kittens stayed in the cat room day after day. I waited patiently by the door, listening to their meows, hoping one day they'd be ready to play with me.

A few weeks later, the kittens were allowed out. I stayed very still as they sniffed my fur, batted my ears, and then pounced on me. **They liked me!**

Together, we invented the coolest games: Pounce Attack, Hide and Squeak, Ear Gliding, and Tail Surfing. I knew they were still recovering, so I was always very careful with them and **NEVER** used my teeth.

Sniff

Sniff

Hooray! I finally had not one, but two new best friends. The humans even called me the best foster brother ever! I didn't know what "foster" meant, but I knew I was happy.

The autumn leaves were falling when the box with the holes came back out. Mom put the kittens in the box and told me that they had been adopted. It turns out that fostering meant we were just taking care of them until they were strong enough to go to their forever home.

After the kittens left, I didn't want to play fetch. I didn't want to eat my dinner. I didn't even run away when Big Red hissed at me.

I was happy they had found a forever home, but without my kittens who would be my friend and playmate?

Luckily, Christmas was right around the corner to cheer me up. My family loves decorating so much, they even decorated us!

But the best part was the beautiful Christmas tree. We have to keep all of the ornaments at the very top, because *someone* just can't control himself.

On Christmas Eve, Mom and Dad brought home another wriggly box with holes in it. What was in the box this time? Was it another foster? I stayed away from it. I didn't want to be sad again.

When Mom opened the box, out jumped the weirdest puppy I had ever seen. She almost looked like me, but she was orange and white and her ears were so long, they flopped around everywhere. Weirdest of all, her nose was pink!

The pink-nosed puppy spent all of
Christmas Eve running around
the house with my sister, bumping into
everything. She sniffed every present under the tree and
even licked a few of them. Gross! My sister laughed and
laughed, but I still kept my distance.

After we put the finishing touches on our giant gingerbread house, it was time for bed. I curled up on my big bed in the kitchen and guess who curled up in a cat bed right next to me: the pink-nosed puppy!

In the middle of the night, I awoke to soft whimpering. Before long, the whimpering turned into whining, then barking, then a full out wolf howl. **What a racket!**

When Mom came over to investigate, I pretended I was sleeping. But I couldn't help but open my eyes when she tucked the pink-nosed puppy in right next to me. She wriggled around, did a little baby yawn, and fell fast asleep.

That's when I knew I was stuck. But she was warm and cozy, so I decided to let her sleep with me just this once. Anything to stop the howling. Besides, I didn't know how long she was going to stay anyway.

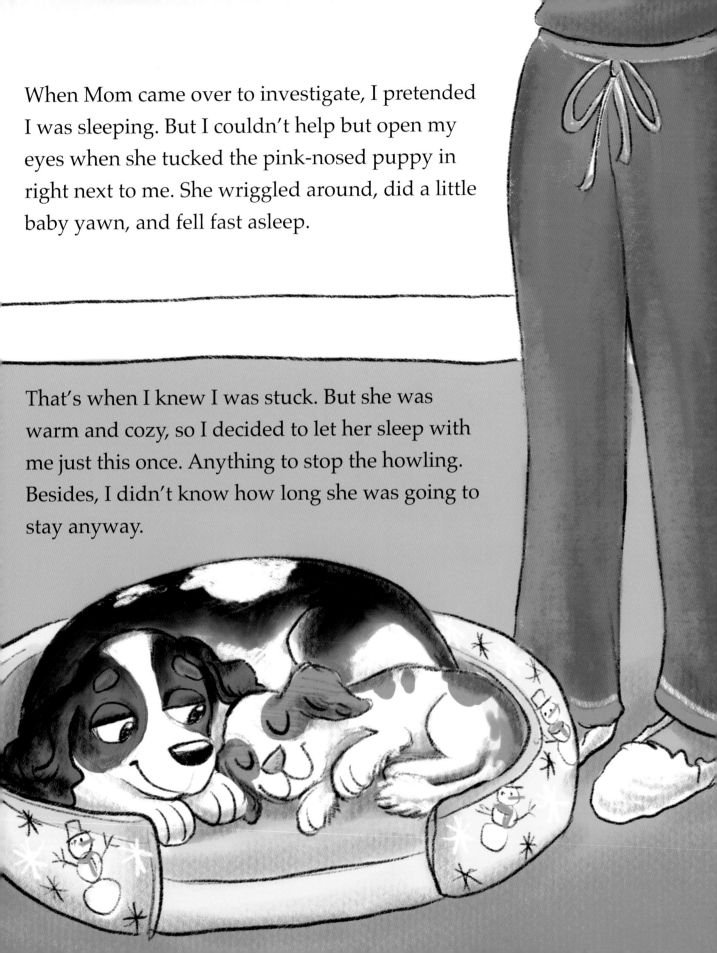

It's Christmas morning! The pink-nosed puppy slept the rest of the night and kept me nice and warm. Just as we crawled out of bed, Big Red came by and boy, did he look grumpy. But she marched up to him and gave him a great big smooch right on his face. He never saw it coming! I had to admit, the kid has guts.

Next was yard patrol. I always sniff carefully as I make my rounds and just as I was sniffing a particularly good scent, someone pounced on my tail. It's that pink-nosed puppy again! I turned around and she nipped at my ears then attacked. Well, she wanted to play and I had been wanting a playmate, so I jumped right back. Cowabunga!

After wrestling the whole morning, we curled up together under the Christmas tree while everyone opened presents. It was so fun having a friend to share Christmas with. I was starting to like this pink-nosed puppy. I hoped she'd stay longer than my kitten playmates.

Suddenly, Dad came over and said, "Let's take a photo of Darcy and his new baby sister Daisy so we can show everybody our new Christmas puppy!"

I couldn't believe it. Daisy was here for good.
It was the best Christmas ever.

And that's the story of how I finally got
the playmate I always wanted!

This is a true story!

Darcy and Daisy are not only brother and sister, they're best friends. Daisy grew up to be a sturdy dog about the same size as Darcy. Her nose eventually filled in completely black. They love going on big adventures, and Daisy still steals kisses whenever she can.

What are Darcy and Daisy doing right now?

They are probably snuggled together after
a playful day to take a cozy nap.

Are you more like Darcy or Daisy?

Answer each question:

1. Would you rather take a long walk or a long nap?
    A walk   **B** nap

2. Do you like loud crazy toys that make a lot of noise?
    A no   **B** yes

3. Do you like meeting new people or are you shy?
    A meet new people   **B** shy

4. Do you like taking baths?
    A yes   **B** no

5. Do you like giving kisses to everyone in your family?
    A no   **B** yes

6. Do you like being near your parents all the time or do you like being by yourself?
    A with parents   **B** by yourself

7. Do you like warming yourself in the sun?

    A no   **B** yes

8. Do you like getting wet in the rain?

    A yes   **B** no

9. What sounds more fun?

    A playing fetch with a ball   **B** playing tug with a toy

If your answers are mostly **A**s then you are like athletic and adventurous **Darcy**.

If your answers are mostly **B**s then you are more like fun-loving and affectionate **Daisy**.

Here are Darcy and Daisy with their friends from the story!

About the Author

Karin Hoving loves making television documentaries because of all the unique experiences they allow her. As a TV producer, she's cuddled with baby chimps, helped excavate dinosaur bones, and filmed at an active volcano. She's pursued giant tarantulas in the Amazon, wrangled a robot competition in Sweden, and herded giant tortoises in the Galápagos Islands. She has edited hundreds of television programs about many different subjects, including giant pandas, UFOs, fashion models, and even Christmas decorating!

Karin lives with her husband and daughter, two funny cats, a sweet hamster, and, of course, two adorable dogs named Darcy and Daisy. This is her first children's book.